I0518716

Christmas Prom Rerun

judythe morgan

Christmas Prom Rerun
Copyright 2023 Hixson RLT

ALL RIGHTS RESERVED. No part of this book, with the exception of brief quotations for book reviews or critical articles, may be reproduced or transmitted in any form or by any means, electronic or mechanical, including photocopying, recording, or by any information storage and retrieval system without express written permission from the author.

Published by The Danfield Press
Contact: www.judythemorgan.com

Cover Design by Jim Peto

Interior Formatting by
Bravia Books

This is a work of fiction. Names, characters, places, and incidents are the product of the author's imagination or are used fictitiously, and any resemblance to actual persons, living or dead, business establishments, events, or locales is entirely coincidental.

ISBN: 978-1-7365539-6-1
First printing

Published in the United States of America.

Dedication

*To everyone with Christmas prom memories,
and for those who think they have none,
may this story bring some.*

*And, for my high school drill team sponsor who
taught me to count steps between yard lines
and so much more. My memories of her
fueled this story.*

Christmas Prom Rerun

Chapter One

Funny how life changes our plans.

Shannon O'Leary pasted a smile on her face and took the seat next to Ashley, a new teacher she'd just met, in her old high school auditorium. The wooden seats were still as hard as ever and the scent of pine floor cleaner used on the stage floor was still as strong. Her eyes scanned back and forth across the room. The district-wide teacher's in-service filled the place where once she'd attended concerts and performed in plays. Her stomach clenched like she was in a vice. This, her gaze swept the room again, this had never been her plan.

Her goal had been to be a celebrity personal trainer. Or coach for an Olympic gymnastics team.

Rich and famous. Instead, here she was divorced and financially desperate, coaching at her old high school and living with her parents. Again. She sucked in a defeated sigh.

"We're so lucky to be here. Superintendent Evans seems so nice." Ashley gushed with a first-year teacher's excitement.

Lucky? Not how Shannon felt. She'd said she'd starve before being a teacher and had only taken education courses to placate her parents. Now it was teach or starve thanks to her ex and her own stupidity. She promised herself this step back wouldn't be for long. She'd leave Dawson Springs once she was debt free and back on her feet.

"Bud…" *Oops,* she swallowed. The superintendent was her godfather. At work, she needed to remember to call him Dr. Evans. "I mean, Dr. Evans is quite proud of our reputation. All alumni are. We were one of the first public school districts in Texas."

"You went to school here?"

"In this very building."

"And now you're teaching here. How wild is that?"

Awkward was more like it. Shannon had dated Tyler Evans, Superintendent Evan's son, all through high school and most of college. She'd ghosted him after the owner of the fitness center noticed her during her internship. Starry-eyed and naive, she'd fallen for all Eric Dewey's lies. And here she sat in the leftover mess of her life gone wrong.

No need to bore Ashley with all that detail. They'd just met. Shannon sat back. Her fingers gripped the wooden arm of the auditorium seat. "Very wild."

"Welcome, teachers. It's going to be an awesome year." Dr. Evans' voice carried from the stage interrupting their conversation.

Shannon shifted her focus to him. A vision of sitting beside Tyler on the same stage during a debate floated through her head. He'd rubbed her shoulder as she rose for her round. The touch gave her the extra confidence she needed at that moment. Her lips tingled recalling the victory kiss afterward. She rubbed her forehead to squish the memories swirling inside. The sound of applause drew her from the past to the present.

"And now I'll turn the program over to my assistant to talk about schedules, transportation, and safety."

Clapping, Shannon stood with the others though she hadn't heard a word her father's best friend had said.

Over the next two hours, Shannon learned more about school operations than she ever dreamed. Some things weren't much different than running a gym. Others, she'd never realized what her teachers at Dawson Springs High had done.

After boxed lunches in the cafeteria, she walked with Ashley down the hallway toward the gym. Ashley turned toward the English department. "Wanna grab something to eat after we finish?"

"Let me see how much I get done. I want the gym set up before I leave today." Shannon hoped that sounded legitimate. Even if she finished, eating out was no longer in her budget.

"I understand. All that equipment. It's a big job. You've got my number. Give me a call if you want to join me." Sincerity rang in Ashley's voice, something Shannon hadn't heard much when she was in the city.

Too bad she'd been too focused on success to pay attention until too late. Like Eric, her attention had been on securing more clients and whatever kept them at their gym. Look where that had gotten her.

Midway through the afternoon, the secretary's voice boomed from the PA, "The building will be closing in one hour, time to start cleaning up."

Shannon scanned the equipment room. Another hour or so and she'd have the inventory finished and everything ready for classes. She set her clipboard on the bin of basketballs and headed to the office to plead her case to stay longer in person. Ms. Castle had always been quick to grant her favors when she'd been a student. She'd let her stay to finish.

Shannon stopped dead in her tracks when Tyler, aka the Superintendent's son, appeared in the gym doorway. With his shoulder against the doorjamb, he blocked the exit.

"Hey, Shannon." His smile grew until it filled her entire field of vision. She blinked. The smile was still there. The faint crow's feet were new, but deep dimples dotted each cheek at the edge of his jaw whiskers.

A rush of euphoria swam through her veins at the sight of him. Five years had only improved his looks. Her hands closed to fists pushing her nails into her palms as she struggled to keep her hormones under control.

He pushed from the wall, inching closer with his same confident swagger. Her feet wouldn't move as he came closer with those dreamy sky-blue eyes zeroing in on hers. Men should not be allowed to have such gorgeous eyes. Her heart pounded like a marching band drummer. Same as it had done whenever he'd come close all through high school and college.

"Hey, yourself." The words squeaked out around the tennis ball lump in her throat.

Tyler rubbed his neck and looked around the empty gym like he didn't know what to say. "Sorry, I haven't come 'round sooner. I've been up in Oklahoma working on a project."

No wonder it'd been so easy to avoid him since she arrived six weeks ago. Not that she even expected him to want to see her after she'd been such a world-class jerk to him.

"I just got home this afternoon," he continued. "Mom told me you'd taken the P.E. teacher's position. Dad is so glad you did." He stopped in front of her. "I was sorry to hear about your divorce."

She inhaled a deep breath waiting for the *I warned you not to marry him.*

"But I'm mighty happy you're back again." His voice softened without a hint of *I told you so.*

She stood straighter. At five foot two, she barely reached his chest. He must have grown another six inches, or the more mature body-builder chest bulging beneath the black t-shirt made him seem bigger than life. She had no idea whether artists worked out or not, but then Tyler had never fit any stereotypical mold and obviously still worked out like he had when he'd been their high school's star athlete.

He'd excelled in football, basketball, and baseball. Ended up accepting a football scholarship at a smaller, nearby state university that also had an award-winning art department. Art was Tyler's heart, and his mom had a wall full of blue ribbons to attest to his talent.

"Thank you." She sidestepped him. "Ms. Castle just announced they're locking the building soon. I need to see if it's okay if I stay and finish the inventory."

"I can hang around and help."

Not a good idea. She didn't need these familiar vibes thrumming through her body. "That's not necessary. Don't you have to get home to someone?"

"Nope. No wife. No girlfriend. Still single. Lost the one I wanted." He winked and heat warmed her cheeks, and if she were honest, her heart. "I'm your slave for however long you need me."

But more time alone with him would only bring more memories and stir feelings she didn't need right now. Her focus had to be on her job and saving up for a place of her own. "I'm good, but thanks."

"Come on. Let me help. It'll go faster." He had that determined set to his jaw.

She cratered. "The clipboard's over there. I'll be right back."

Chapter Two

Tyler stared as Shannon disappeared down the hallway with her auburn ponytail swishing. *Hold on, buddy. This isn't high school anymore.* She probably isn't ready for another relationship, even if he was. He needed to slow down. Give her time to recoup before he tries to win her back.

He hadn't been able to think, let alone paint that first year after she'd fallen for the jerk who was her intern sponsor. Eric Dewey took advantage of her and for that, Tyler would never forgive him. Well, she was finally back at home where she belonged, and he wouldn't give up easily again.

He'd loved Shannon O'Leary from the moment she joined the debate team in middle school. All sass and facts. As far as he was concerned, love was forever. She'd said she loved him once. He believed she could love him again. He just had to convince her. He slapped the clipboard to his thigh and walked into the equipment room.

Shannon's quick trip to the office took forever. Ms. Castle, the school administrative assistant, gushed on and on about how happy she was to have Shannon back and filled her in on the last five years' worth of gossip before she could ask about staying late.

Ms. C cocked her lip in a grimace. "I don't know. I'm not supposed to let anyone stay alone in the building after four. You're the only one who's asked."

"I won't be alone. Tyler's with me." The words slipped out before Shannon could stop them. "He's helping. With two of us, it won't be much longer."

"I still have to ask—"

"So, you two have taken up where you left off then?" Mrs. Atkins, Shannon's former science teacher and now the school principal came from her office behind Ms. C. Her pursed lips scrunched her face into a disapproving scowl. "Better not catch you making out like you used to do in the science equipment room."

"We're not ...he just stopped by to say hello and offered to help ..." Shannon clamped her lips shut.

Pointless to argue, neither woman was listening, too focused on trying to best each other with bygone tales about her and Tyler.

Ms. C. chuckled. "One time Bud was at a principals' meeting and Shannon talked me into letting them go off campus for lunch. Bud surprised them by stopping at the same place. He was not happy."

"I would have liked to have been a fly on the wall when Tyler got home that night." Mrs. Atkins gave her legendary cackling laugh.

"This is not the same thing. I want to stay so I can have everything ready when classes start. Please. I will lock the gym up when I leave. I'll be doing it after football games anyway." She pulled her key from her pocket and dangled it. "See."

"Okay. Fine." Mrs. Adkins nodded. "You two were so sweet together. Any chance you will get back together?"

"No. We've both moved on." Shannon returned her very best smile. This trip down memory lane needed to end. "Thank you so much."

She heard the ball bouncing as she neared the gym and paused at the doorway. Tyler arched for a free throw looking as good as he had at seventeen. Her breath froze somewhere between the past and present making her pulse stutter like it was freefalling off a cheerleader pyramid. How was she going to make it through living in the same town with him when her self-control slipped a little more each time she saw him?

"We're good," she said as the ball swished through the net.

Scooping up the ball, he fired it into the storage bin and picked up the clipboard. "All equipment's accounted for. Down to the last yellow Pickleball." He passed her the completed lists.

The sensation of his warm, smooth fingertips against hers made her grip unsteady. The clipboard wobbled. He squeezed her hand in his to steady the board before it fell. She felt a tremor that matched hers.

Whoa. Time out. He has no reason to care anymore. Not after what you did to him.

She hugged the board to her chest. "I really hadn't intended to be gone for so long. Ms. C wanted to fill me in on all the gossip, past and present."

"She's a talker, according to Dad. I didn't expect you back very quickly."

"Mrs. Adkins had to chime in too. Can you believe she's the principal?"

"Her appointment was a shocker. The woman was a slave driver in the classroom. I hope she's not that way with teachers."

Shannon cringed. She'd never really thought about that possibility. "I sure hope not too."

"You'll do fine. What's left to do?"

"Inspect the lockers and set up my office, but I can do those. You've done enough."

"Together we'll finish in no time. You take care of your office. I've got the lockers." He headed to the boys' locker room.

Tyler hadn't changed. He'd always been kind and helpful. Considerate. Unlike Eric who'd watched her heft heavy mats while he chatted up female clients at their gym.

A short time later, she met Tyler coming from the locker room. "All done," he said and gave her a high-five clap. "How 'bout we go grab a burger at Smitty's?"

Unbidden, another surge of nostalgia hit her. So many times, they'd gone for burgers after practices and games. No more, those days were gone forever. Their history was just that … history. Besides, eating out was an indulgence she couldn't afford. Not if she wanted to save enough for a deposit on a place of her own. None of the artists she knew made much money. Eating out was likely a luxury for him too.

"Thanks, but no. I need to get back out to the ranch. Mom's waiting supper." She pushed the heavy gym door open. It closed with a bang. Using her key, she locked it and headed to her car.

Tyler trailed behind her. He patted the roof of her vintage Dodge Charger once shiny silver now faded to smoky blue gray with splotches of bare metal. "I figured old Bessie had been sent to the scrap yard long ago."

"Mom and Dad kept her in one of the ranch sheds. She's great for driving around here. She'd never have made it in the city traffic. I had to sell my BMW." The glossy black BMW had zoomed through the heavy city traffic, but she couldn't afford the payment on her teacher's salary. If she were honest, she didn't miss it or what the car and what driving it would have reminded her of. Better it was gone. Bessie got her where she needed to go, most of the time.

He winced. "BMW, huh? Still about the bright lights and fine things with you."

Her wanting to escape the small town he loved for a bigger life in the city was always a sore spot between them. If only she'd listened to him, she wouldn't be back, eating her words.

She should be the one wincing. Regret was a bitter pill to swallow. "Thanks for all your help today."

"Be seeing you around."

Chapter Three

The debacle of her life ran through her head as Shannon drove home. Try as she may, she couldn't turn off Eric's voice in her head convincing her they needed to invest more and more in the gym.

"We have a consistent 18–25-year-old clientele, but we need to upgrade the equipment to appeal to the 55+ crowd."

"If we added a steam room in both locker rooms ..."

"We need a juice bar ..."

She'd been too naïve to question anything he'd said and let him talk her into every improvement and signing order after order with his assurances that upgrades would bring in more customers.

When that didn't happen, she taught more dance and aerobics classes and began an after-school kids' program to cover the loan payments. Giving him credit where credit was due, Eric offered private training sessions. Still, it was never enough to meet their expenses.

In the end, she'd gone back to teaching in public school to keep their heads above water. Barely. The debt mounted. They argued constantly.

One night she'd gone to the gym to apologize after a major fight. What she found was a vision she'd never be able to unsee. Him, butt-naked, on the locker room bench wrapped around Sylvie Howard, a workout client, and her *"best"* friend. Her knuckles whitened around the steering wheel. They'd been cheating for years. Tears welled. She'd been such a fool.

Bessie's headlights shined on the two-hundred-year-old oak marking the entrance for Irish Oaks. She straightened her spine and forced the remembrances into the dark dungeons of her mind where they belonged. The cattle guard bumpety-bumped beneath her tires.

Her mom waved from the wrap-around porch of the 1930s ranch home that had belonged to her paternal grandparents. The comfort she'd always known in this place soothed her angst.

Here she could trust the ones she loved.

She parked Bessie and headed inside. Her mom opened the screen door. "Dad and I ate early, but I have a plate waiting for you. Put your stuff away and come to the kitchen. You can tell me all about your day. Daddy's checking on a momma cow."

What she wanted to do was take a long jog to sweat the sight of Tyler and the rise of old feelings out of her system. She couldn't bring herself to say no to her mom. "Sounds like a plan."

When she came back downstairs, her mom set a plate filled with pot roast, new potatoes, carrots, and celery with fresh-picked green beans at her place and slid into the chair across from her.

"I saw Marilyn Evans at the grocery store this afternoon."

Ah-ha! No wonder Tyler had come to help her. Their moms were up to their old matchmaker tricks. "Tyler stopped by the school and helped me do inventory in the gym."

Her mom's eyes lit up and a smile dimpled her cheeks. "That was nice of him. He's never married, you know." She wanted to pretend things hadn't changed. That Tyler and Shannon could end up together.

After Eric, Shannon didn't believe in fairy tale endings anymore. Or want one. She was happy the two mothers had mended the breach in their friendship her marrying Eric had caused, but the matchmaking had to be nipped in the bud. That was over and done.

Reaching across the table, she took her mom's hand. She kept her voice smooth and her frustration in check. Despite her best efforts, an edge still grated in her voice when she spoke. "I love you, and Dad. You've taken me in and are helping me get on my feet again, but you have to understand, I'm not interested in reliving the past or starting over with Tyler. Or any man for that matter. Not after Eric's shenanigans."

Her mom squeezed Shannon's hand. "I prefer to believe in possibilities." Her words rang with disappointment as she pushed from the round oak table that had been in the big kitchen since Shannon was a baby. "How 'bout some pie?"

"Thanks, but no. I need to get lesson plans ready. With all the drill team and cheerleaders' practices, I haven't even had time to go over the curriculum guide."

Bud had assigned her sponsorship duties for the drill team and cheerleaders. She was grateful. The extra stipends would help her get on her feet faster. Managing the cheerleaders would be a piece of cake. She'd spent enough years as one, but coaching the drill team? She didn't know a thing about precision drill patterns. Thank goodness the band director did.

Chapter Four

The first weeks of any school year were always hard. New students to learn and new routines to set up. Shannon learned that when she'd taken the teaching job to keep their health club afloat. This year was no exception and being back in her hometown added extra stress. Since she'd returned, Dawson Springs' small-town 5G wireless gossip network was crazy with rumors and twisted facts. Too many teachers had taught her and too many parents had been her classmates.

Every day was a minefield. As hard as she tried to put the past behind her, forgetting was impossible. Someone constantly shared how they remembered when she and Tyler had been a couple followed by, do you think you'll ever get back together?

The drill team added more pressure. After weeks of 5:30 a.m. summer practices, they still couldn't count the sixteen steps between yard lines. Shannon stood on the sideline watching Thursday afternoon practice the first week of classes. Their lines writhed like a snake. She gnawed the cuticle on her thumb. Their first performance was in two weeks and it did not look good.

With a frustrated shiver, she blew her whistle to stop the girls and jogged out onto the field. "You are going to have to stay in a straight line."

"But Ms. O'Leary. my legs are just too short," Julie whined.

Shannon sucked in a slow breath. She didn't need another call from Julie's mom, but the girl had to get her act together. Julie marched at the end of the line of officers. If she were off step, it would be too obvious.

"You're not that much shorter than me. You can do this. Stretch your leg like this." Shannon took the position at the end of the officers and demonstrated one more time how to take wider steps and keep their shoulders lined up. She walked with her through the whole maneuver.

Julie gave her a double thumbs up as they finished the routine. "I think I have it now. Thank you."

During the last practice before the game, the

drills continued to resemble a rat's maze, and thinking about their halftime performance made Shannon's head hurt. There was one tricky sequence in tonight's show where the drill team sidestepped through the band lines. Not once had they gotten it right during practice. With every execution, a trombone slammed into someone's shoulder or a hip banged a snare drum because someone wasn't lined up correctly. Granted, it wasn't always the drill team's fault. Sometimes a band member misstepped.

Shannon envisioned a major disaster during halftime with all the parents watching, including hers, and Superintendent Evans.

By Friday morning's schoolwide pregame pep rally, her stomach twisted in a knot. She waited to lead the drill team inside.

Holly, the head cheerleader, walked by. Her shoulders slumped. Her swollen red eyes looked like she hadn't slept at all.

Shannon pulled her off to the side. "What on earth happened to you?"

Holly burst into tears. "Brock and I broke up."

Shannon inhaled a deep breath. A teenage girl's worst calamity. The sleepless nights the summer she and Tyler broke up kicked around in her head. The hurt and pain had felt like the end of the world.

She took Holly's hand in hers. "I'm so sorry. Breakups hurt. I'm sure you and Brock will work things out."

"I love Brock." Holly pulled away and swiped her hand at a fresh tear trailing over her cheek. "I hope you're right."

"I know I am." She and Tyler had always been miserable apart. So miserable, they'd quickly gotten back together. Only to break up for good after she met Eric. How foolish she'd been.

Her pep talk didn't do Holly much good. Her pep rally cheers were lackluster, and she flubbed her last backflip.

Since Holly's boyfriend just happened to be the star quarterback, Shannon cornered Coach Martin later in the day and let him know about the breakup. She hoped he'd have better luck keeping his player focused than she was having with her head cheerleader and the drill team's marching.

By kickoff on Friday night, Holly seemed better, but the makeup she'd applied with a shovel didn't conceal her puffy eyes. The drill team girls were pumped on the bus ride to the game, assuring her they had it. Shannon crossed her fingers.

As the first half ended, she prayed for the best. The girls lined up under the far goalposts. The band at the near end of the field.

She pressed her knuckles to her cheek and gnawed at the skin on the inside of her mouth when the drum major raised his baton for the band and drill team to march onto the field.

*

Tyler's mom nudged his shoulder with hers. "You should go sit with Shannon and watch her first show with her."

Nothing he would like better, but Shannon had avoided him since he'd helped her set up the gym. With both his parents being schoolteachers, he recognized the first six weeks were always tough. He'd experienced the stress firsthand. Wanting to give Shannon some space to get her feet under her, he'd put Operation Win Shannon Back on hold.

"I'm not sure it's a good idea."

"I think she'd welcome the support. She's worried it's going to be a disaster." Shannon's mother glanced at Tyler's father sitting on the other side of his mother. "Pretend you didn't hear that, Bud."

His dad chuckled. "Understood. They'll do fine. Knowing she has your support would be nice, son. Like old times."

Tyler didn't want to get into it with his parents. Anything that might or might not happen between him and Shannon was private.

Fat chance of that, he chuckled under his breath. Private and small towns did not go together. At all.

He glanced over to the empty section where the band and drill team had been sitting. Even from this distance, he could feel her tension. Shannon's thumb pushed into her cheek, nibbling the inside of her mouth. A telltale sign she was nervous or worried.

Truthfully, he could understand her worry. He'd driven by the practice field more than once and seen the spaghetti lines crisscrossing one another. He was worried too.

He should go comfort her now, before the disaster. Let her know he'd be there for her.

Shannon jumped when a hand rested on her shoulder and Tyler slid down beside her on the bleachers.

He gently pulled her hand from her cheek. "Relax."

She didn't want to accept the comfort, but his hand in hers offered a reassurance she'd missed. She focused her attention on the field.

The drill team and band started the slide movement. She slid her hand from his, squeezed her eyes shut, and pressed her hands to her cheeks.

Tyler whispered into her ear and lowered her hands. "You can open your eyes. They're doing great."

She opened her eyes to tiny slits. Her girls passed through the band players' lines without a single misstep. "They did it!" She jumped from her seat clapping and hugged Tyler.

He lifted her in the air and swung her back and forth like a clock pendulum. "Congratulations."

Having his arms around her melted the last trace of drill team anxiety and sent a swarm of fireflies fluttering and glowing inside her chest. Their faces were mere inches apart. His eyes drifted to her lips. The stadium noises faded. Old feelings tingled between them. She thought for sure he was going to kiss her. She didn't move though she should. At the last second, he sank onto the stadium bench with her.

The unexpected gush of disappointment dowsed the fireflies. What was wrong with her? They weren't in high school anymore. She stiffened and pulled herself back to the here and now and watched her girls and the band members march off the field.

"I can't believe they did it."

"I wasn't sure they could pull it off either."

She gave him a questioning look.

"I may have watched your practices once or twice," he said with a grin.

She chuckled. "They were a mess."

"But they came through. Good job, you!" He cupped her into his shoulder.

Leaning out of his embrace, she watched Holly lead the cheerleaders back to the stands from their break with as much enthusiasm as Joan of Arc heading to the stake. "I wish I could perk Holly up."

"What's wrong?"

"She and Brock broke up. When you're a teen, that feels like the end of the world."

He turned to face her again, his voice filled with memory. "Breaking up at any age is never easy."

She knew he didn't mean Brock and Holly. She agreed, but then she'd been extremely happy to be free of Eric.

Silence stretched.

Finally, Tyler blinked and took a deep breath. "At least the breakup explains Brock's missed plays. Being two touchdowns behind isn't too bad, but Coach needs to get that boy's mind back in the game. Otherwise, we're going to lose."

The drill team started up the aisle. Tyler patted Shannon's thigh and stood. "Great half-time show, Shannon."

Descending the bleachers' steps, he slapped palms with the returning girls along the way.

"Good-looking boyfriend you got there, Ms. O'Leary." The drill team captain slid into the spot he'd vacated beside Shannon.

"He's just an old friend."

"Are you sure? Didn't look like that to me." The senior girl gave a knowing wink and took her place with the rest of the squad.

Chapter Five

Shannon gave the drill team and cheerleaders Monday practice off. They deserved it and she needed the break. She sat at her desk going over the band directions for next week's formations.

"I hear you canceled practice."

Shannon looked up, ignoring the uptick in her heartbeat to see Tyler. "I did and I'm hoping I didn't make a mistake."

"The girls deserve a day off." He sauntered toward her desk. "I'm thinking the teacher should have a break too. Let's go someplace for lunch and celebrate the victory that didn't look like it would happen."

Tempting, but not wise for so many reasons. She thought she'd seen something in Tyler's eyes

Friday night at the game and the same something echoed through her. "Tyler, I can't leave campus in the middle of the day. You know the rules."

Coach Martin scooted from his desk as the bell rang. A smile covered his square bulldog face. "Go on. Go with him. I'll cover for you."

"Thanks, Coach. See, no excuse now." Tyler reached out, took her hand, and tugged her from her desk chair.

And she let him.

She shouldn't. She didn't want to send the wrong message, but she hadn't had a break since school started and next week's formations looked like one of her mother's counted cross-stitch patterns. "Where are we going?"

"You'll see."

A companionable silence rode with them as his old truck, the same one he'd had when they'd dated, rattled and creaked down Dawson Springs' Main Street. Living in the center of things in a large metropolitan city, she'd forgotten the quiet and beauty of her hometown. The courthouse stood like a gothic fortress in the center of town square. Shop names were different from when she'd lived here. So were the landscape plants. Dawson Springs had changed.

Yet it hadn't, and the longer she was here the more she realized how much she'd missed it. And Tyler.

Shannon had a good idea of their destination

when he took the road out of town toward the state park. That had been their dating go-to location when they had no money to go anywhere else. He drove passed the turnoff.

"We're not going to the park?"

"I know you love it there and I'm guessing you haven't been since you got back, but I've got someplace else in mind."

"There didn't use to be anything beyond the park. Are they developing out here now?"

"No. Most of the land next to the park is still privately owned. I don't see the owner selling out."

The truck crested the rise and the soft rolling landscape unfurled before them. Mesquite and Yaupon trees dotted the fields of the Texas hill country. Cactus fanned in clusters. Some with fading blooms. Tyler turned onto a gravel road then pulled over after going a short distance. He leaned his chin on the steering wheel. "Ranchers do like their wide-open spaces and so do I."

"I bet it's gorgeous in the springtime covered in bluebonnets and Indian paintbrushes."

"Beyond words. It's my favorite place to paint. Shall we?" He reached behind her and grabbed a picnic basket. His aftershave sent a minty scent to tickle her nose. In high school, he'd used a woodsy scent. The new scent suited him.

Together they flapped the blanket open, parachuting it to the ground, and sat on either side of the picnic basket.

He handed her a sandwich. "PB and grape jelly. I hope that's still your favorite. Chocolate chip cookies. Probably not as good as yours. And a diet Coke." He held the can high.

Not the fancy food she'd eaten with Eric at those swanky restaurants but all her favorites. She took a bite of the sandwich. "How'd you find this place?"

"The landowner's a friend. I can set up my easel wherever I want."

"You're still painting?"

"Yep. Mostly on canvas now. Houses occasionally."

"I'm so glad. You were too good to ever stop." She smiled at him. A second time she saw and felt the same dangerous sensation she'd experienced at the game.

"Landscapes mostly. Some portraits when someone asks. Speaking of which, I still have the one I did for you. You think you'll want it back once you're in a place of your own? I've kept it for you."

"I never want it back." She sucked in a breath. "Sorry, I didn't mean that like it sounded." She'd loved that painting of her on the porch swing until Eric ripped if off the wall during one of their nastier arguments. He'd stormed out and returned it to Tyler. That's all she'd see now when she looked at it. "I don't want anything that reminds me of him or that time."

"I can understand. I remember the ugly scene when he returned it. I only kept it for you. I'll just keep using it as a sample at shows."

"I would like to see some of your landscapes. Maybe buy one of those."

"Come by my place anytime and you can pick one. No charge." He winked and stretched out on the blanket with his hands behind his head. "Remember how we used to challenge each other to find things in the cloud formations."

"Like that horse up there?" She pointed to the sky.

"Nah, that's not a horse. It's a lion. See how its mane goes around his head?"

"Uh-uh. It's the rider hugging his horse's neck." Shannon chuckled. She loved how easy it was to be with him.

"No way."

The game went on for a few minutes. One spying something and the other disputing as they watched the clouds float in the sky. Shannon sighed. "I could do this all afternoon, but I don't want Mrs. Atkins to catch us. We better head back."

When he dropped her off at the gym, he squeezed her hand. "I enjoyed this afternoon. We'll have to do it again. Soon."

The prudent thing to do was to say *no* to discourage whatever this was between them. But the afternoon had been fun. Relaxing. Comfortable like old times. Spending time with him, renewing their friendship, what could it hurt?

"We'll see." She nodded and slid from his truck.

Ashley caught up to her in the teacher's parking lot after school. "You left campus with Dr. Evans' son? You forget what happened last time?"

Shannon shivered. Ashley had heard that story. The gossip mill struck again. "It was okay. Coach Martin covered for me, and I was only gone for lunch. Okay, it might have been sixth period when we got back. How'd you find out?"

"One of my students saw you get into an old pickup and asked. I told her you were on a school errand."

"Thanks."

"You'd do the same for me."

Ashely was right. She'd become a good friend, without the baggage of Shannon's other friends in Dawson Springs. "I would."

"So, where'd you two go? Not the diner where Dr. Evans eats, I hope."

Shannon shook her head. "Tyler brought a picnic lunch. I'm not sure where we went. Some ranch. It was so beautiful and peaceful."

Ashley cocked her head. "His?"

"Don't think so. Just someplace he sometimes goes to paint." She tucked her bag tighter on her shoulder. "I'll see you tomorrow."

"Whoa. Not so fast." Ashely stepped in front of her, blocking her retreat. "Are you two hooking up again?"

"No. We're friends. That's all." Shannon ducked around her, thankful they'd reached old Bessie. "It's late. I need to get home."

"Okay, but you deserve a good relationship after what happened with Eric. Why not him?"

"Not happening." That possibility disappeared years ago, and she wasn't getting into more discussion.

Shannon opened her car door and tossed her gym bag into the back seat. "See you tomorrow.

The marching season officially ended after the football team lost their first bi-district playoff game. Her nails testified that she barely survived her very first football season as drill team sponsor. But the nails might grow again and the dark circles under her eyes should disappear now that there were no half-time performances to worry about.

Except, the end of the season also meant her next big responsibility was fast approaching — the annual Christmas Prom hosted by the cheerleaders and drill team.

But first she had to get through Thanksgiving with her family and the Evans, which meant close contact with Tyler.

The two families began switching host homes for the holiday dinners when she and Tyler were in grade school. Her dumping of him had caused a rift between the longtime friends. Her return, without Eric, had bridged the chasm. The shared dinners were back on. Both mothers reunited with renewed hopes for the happy ever after they wanted for their children.

Thanksgiving would be at the Evans' home this year and Christmas lunch at hers with a gift exchange. Shannon was not looking forward to either holiday. She may have sent the wrong signals at the picnic with Tyler. She was not interested in any relationship. Not until she'd paid off all her debt and maybe not then.

Liar, liar. You're fooling yourself.

She rubbed her neck and opened the file of earlier Christmas proms for ideas. Looking at the pictures of previous dances she'd attended with Tyler almost made her believe again. They looked so happy, the perfect couple.

Too much holiday family time with him could be dangerous. Whenever she was with Tyler old feelings flickered. She'd tried to beg off the Thanksgiving gathering. Her mom wouldn't hear of it. That's why two weeks later, she stared into the Evans' formal dining room unable to take another step.

The ceramic pilgrims and centerpiece had aged over the years. Fresh fall foliage, pumpkins, and gourds surrounded the serving dishes filled to overflowing on the buffet. Crystal glasses sparkled. Silverware glowed. How many years had she and Tyler helped his mom polish and arrange it all?

Mrs. Evans' voice came from the kitchen. "Everyone find their seats. Names are on the place cards."

Lost in the memories of Thanksgiving lunches past, she jumped when Tyler spoke, "A lot of these decorations are older than we are."

"Wait till you see the Christmas tree at our house. You'll recognize the ornaments."

"Some things never change." His gaze held hers.

Tiny basketballs bounced in her stomach. She took a discreet step back, needing space to absorb the sensations both foreign and familiar.

His hand grazed her arm as he motioned her forward. Those orange balls dribbled faster. "This side. No surprise, Mom has us seated together."

She crossed her arms against her chest to calm the accelerated dribbling and took her seat. This was going to be a long day.

A very long day.

Chapter Six

Shannon's cell rang on Sunday night. She swiped when the caller ID read Ashley. "Hi, Ashley. Welcome home."

"So how was your Thanksgiving?" Ashley's voice bubbled.

"I survived. But I don't want to talk about it. Tell me about your cruise."

Shannon held crossed fingers to her lips. *Please let the diversion work.* She'd had enough reliving of that day. All her mother had done was talk about how wonderful it was having everyone together and how great Christmas would be.

"Fan-tab-u-lous. Grenada was the best stop. Not that all the white beaches and turquoise water weren't fabulous. As we landed, I swear I could smell the spices and the House of Chocolate. Oh my god... I mean goodness, sorry. Wait till you taste the samples I bought."

"Chocolate sounds heavenly about now."

"You're the only person I've ever met who isn't into chocolate. If chocolate sounds heavenly, Thanksgiving must have been awful. What happened?"

"Nothing. It's Christmas Prom. So much to do. A theme to decide then get the props made. Thanks for the DJ tip. He's signed up. The girls are so excited. How'd you know about him?"

"Coop, the guy at my apartment that I told you about is the DJ's friend and says he's played for lots of proms. Coop says he'll be great."

"Holly and some of the other girls recognized the name. They are so excited. I owe you."

"Is Dr. Evans' son gonna be at the prom?"

Shannon sucked in a deep breath. "No reason to be. Dr. Evans will be though."

"Shucks, I'd like to meet his son. Listen, I'd love to chat more but I've put off lesson plans as long as I can."

"Me too. Thanks for checking in. Thanksgiving dinner really wasn't that awful, but now I just have to get through prom." She wasn't going to think about the Christmas family gathering yet.

"You'll ace prom. Look how you shaped up the drill team. But I still want to know more about Dr. Evans' son. Me thinks there is more to the guy than you're sharing. Ciao."

More? There'd been too much. Shannon couldn't stop thinking about how attentive he was or how he'd found a gazillion ways to touch her as they passed the serving dishes.

The first week back from Thanksgiving break, the girls chose a Winter Wonderland theme for Christmas prom. Shannon let them submit designs. Then all the girls would vote.

Liz Hemphill, Holly's foster mom, and a former school cheerleader with Shannon, sidetracked her when she came to pick up her daughter from practice.

"Can you believe it? We're working together on Christmas Prom. Just like we did on ours. It's so exciting." Liz rolled her shoulders in and did a little quiver. For as long as Shannon had known her, whenever she got excited or happy or anxious, Liz did a twitch.

"I know, but there's a big difference now. I'm the sponsor and you're the mom of a cheerleader." Shannon hadn't completely wrapped her head around her super self-centered best friend being a single *foster* parent of a teen. She was proud of Liz for stepping up when Holly lost her parents.

"Oh, I know." Another twitch. "It's still déjà vu seeing Holly creating designs with her friends like we used to do. It's so sweet. Have you made your decision on whose design you'll use?"

"Not my decision. The girls vote. Today was the deadline. I'm sure they'll make an excellent choice. See you."

Working on Christmas prom turned out to be more trying than the first days of classes. She didn't need Liz's reminder. Too many memories of other proms already circled in her head.

The drill team and cheerleaders voted for Dickens' holiday village theme, and the real work began. Shannon scheduled afterschool sessions to paint backdrops with scenes, create snowflakes and spray fake trees white, and assemble all the little table decorations. Their remarkably successful fundraiser meant the girls could go all out setting up a faux Dickens village.

One of the dads who ran the building supply in town donated plywood and cut all the shop fronts. Another donated paint. Everyone was into the Dawson Springs High social event, second only to the senior prom. Ashley volunteered to help immediately. She was as excited as the girls.

"Are we going to have the guys help?" Holly asked as soon as Shannon posted the work schedule.

Not surprised by the question, Shannon struck a Woman Wonder pose. "We can manage it ourselves." Glancing down at the massive plywood Christmas village backdrops, she quickly added, "And we'll have teachers and dads to help."

"But our last sponsor let the guys help," Holly protested.

Liz chimed in, "So did ours. Don't you remember how Ms Tuttle caught you and Tyler Evans locking lips at least a dozen times?"

As much as she didn't want to, Shannon did remember and it was the main reason she had vetoed the boys' help this year. Romance reigned at Christmas. She had enough on her plate without all those teenage hormones complicating things. The memories were hard enough to manage.

Holly gave her a sly grin. "He's the one at the first football game, wasn't he? You told Lily you were just friends. I knew there was more to it."

Liz gave a dreamy sigh. "Friends now but I was there and they were the most perfect Winter King and Queen our senior year. We all thought for sure you two would get married."

Shannon quickly waved the electric nail gun. "But that didn't happen. Let's get these braces nailed onto the backboards so we can start painting."

The buzz didn't die down. Shannon quickly came to dread the tulle-netting cutting and backdrop painting sessions.

She scheduled the final decorating session the day before the dance. That freed the day of the dance for the girls to schedule hair and nail appointments and be ready for their dates.

Dads came on Friday afternoon to move props into place, hang tulle, string lights, and set up refreshment tables with remarkable speed. Three hours later, she dimmed the lights for one final check. Oohs and ahhs spread softly.

"It's wonderful." Holly stood back admiring their work. "It's going to be a perfect prom."

"I can't wait for tomorrow night," another drill team member echoed.

Liz squeezed Holly. "Ms. O'Leary and I felt the same way for our prom." She winked at Shannon.

Liz's dream had come true. She'd married her high school sweetheart and had a storybook life. Shannon let hers slip away. "Let's finish cleaning up and head out. It's late."

A short time later, Shannon walked with the girls and workers to the exit. Ashely turned and looked back. "It is marvelous. Makes me wish I had a date. Do teachers bring plus ones?"

"Sure, and there'll be lots of spouses too."

"Too bad I don't have a spouse or a plus one."

"What about Coop?"

Ashley groaned. "No way. Want me to hang around until you close?"

"Nah. I'm good. You go on. I'll see you tomorrow night."

Shannon made one last check around the room before leaving and smiled. The cafeteria did look like a Hallmark set with the fake snow and twinkling lights embedded in the netting. She flipped the switch. Tomorrow night would be a memory-making night for the girls.

Same as hers had been. She shoved the thought away and locked up.

Outside, stars sparkled in the dark sky. A chill in the air had her shivering on her way to her car. She climbed into Bessie and turned the key in the ignition. All she got was a click. Adjusting the gear shift, she pumped the accelerator. Bessie made a grinding sound like she was trying, but the engine wouldn't turn over. When she smelled something burning, she stopped. Her Bessie wasn't going to start.

She checked her watch. Way too late to call her parents. They'd be fast asleep and, if she woke them, she'd get a forty-minute lecture on safety and single women.

No thanks, she did not need that.

Small, rural towns tended to roll up the sidewalks at dark, so probably no late-night tow service to call either. Another reason she'd preferred city life. Life didn't stop at six-thirty p.m.

She leaned back against the headrest debating about who to wake up. Tyler popped into her head. She quickly nixed that idea. She was not going to have him bailing her out. It'd only encourage him.

Ashely would come. But then she'd have more questions about Shannon's relationship with Tyler.

Same reason she nixed Liz. She'd bring Holly and it'd be the inquisition all over again. Shannon had had her fill of questions tonight.

She closed her eyes only for a minute to think. Exhausted, she fell fast asleep.

Chapter Seven

Minutes or hours later, she wasn't sure which, a tap on the car window woke her. She turned to see Tyler's face. Heart pounding, she hopped out. "What are you doing here? You nearly scared me to death."

"Your mother was worried when you didn't get home or call. She asked me to check on you."

How like her mom to seize a matchmaking moment. Irritation coupled with relief and joy like a speeding train spread through her veins.

He looked at the car and back at her paint-dripped clothes. "Uhmmm, why are you sleeping in your car?"

"Bessie wouldn't start. I fell asleep trying to decide who to wake up."

"Call your mother, let her know you're safe. I'll get a flashlight from my truck and see if I can figure out what's wrong."

After reassuring her mother she was fine, Shannon went to stand beside Tyler beneath the raised hood. She'd deal with the matchmaking later.

Tyler's flashlight lit the engine. He shook his head. "It's too dark to see or do much. Why don't I give you a ride home? I'll get Rick to come over and look at Bessie tomorrow."

"Rick's still here too?" Rick Hendrick had been part of their fearsome foursome in high school. His girlfriend Tammy, like Shannon, had gone off to college and married someone else.

Unlike her, Tammy was still married.

"Yep, he ended up marrying Suzanne. Thought you knew that. He'll be able to get Bessie running again." Tyler slammed the hood. "Get what you need and lock her up then give me the keys, and I'll get them to Rick."

She followed him to his pickup. Moonlight highlighted the rust spots. The door gave the telltale squeak when he opened it for her. He wasn't doing any better with his life's plan to be a famous artist than she was with her plan to be a well-paid personal trainer.

So much for plans.

"I hope Rick can fix Bessie."

"He can. He's a whiz at repairing old cars. He's why my truck's still running."

Déjà vu filled the cab on the thirty-minute ride to her parents' ranch. Rattling pickup. Moonbeams shining in. Only this time there was no cuddling or kissing.

Conversation lapsed. Tyler turned on the radio but turned it off again. Nothing much on the airways this late but talk shows and Tejano stations. He probably couldn't afford Satellite radio like she'd had in her BMW. She did miss that.

She clutched her tote to her chest, and Tyler focused on the highway as silence filled the car and windows fogged from the dropping temperatures.

He turned up the oak-lined drive a little too fast. The truck bounced roughly over the cattle guard.

So did Shannon. Her tote nearly tumbled off her lap.

"Sorry. I forgot about that."

"No problem." He'd sped over the grate every time as they'd rushed home to beat her curfew.

He glided to a stop at the front porch, and she opened the door before he could get out. "Thanks for rescuing this damsel in distress."

"Anytime. When I told you I'd always be here for you, I meant it." He smiled. A smile of precious memories, of a love they'd believed could never be broken.

Until she had.

She swallowed the shiver rushing up her spine — from cold or longing she wasn't sure which — and walked up the steps. He waited in the truck, watching.

Without thinking, she flipped the porch light to let him know she was safe inside like she'd done when they'd been dating. The truck headlights flashed across the front of the house as he pulled away.

Shannon peeked out the window to watch his bright red taillights turn onto the highway. Tears blurred the color to bright crimson starbursts. She swiped her cheeks before she went upstairs to her room.

After her shower, she climbed into bed. For a moment she lay in silence. She'd known she'd have to face Tyler when she decided to come back to Dawson Springs. She never expected to see him as much as she was.

Or the odd attraction growing between them. What was that all about?

She punched the pillow. Whatever it was had to stop.

Liar, liar. Her conscience taunted.

The next morning Rick called. "Bessie needs a new alternator, and parts for old cars aren't easy to find. Until I can find one, she's not drivable. I'm sorry."

"It's okay. There are only three days of school left next week before the Christmas holiday break, I can manage."

Except for Christmas Prom that night. She'd have to hitch a ride into town with her folks who had a party at church. She called Ashley for a ride home. "Hey, girlfriend. I need a favor."

"Sure. Anything after all you've done to help me get through the semester. Whatcha need?" Shannon filled Ashley in on Bessie's problems. "I knew I should have stayed and helped you finish up last night."

"It's no big deal. I got home fine." No way was she mentioning Tyler came to her rescue. Ashley would be all over that. "My parents have a Christmas party in town tonight so I can hitch a ride to the dance with them, but I'll need a ride home after. Do you mind?"

"Not at all."

"I was getting worried," Ashley greeted Shannon when she hopped out of her parents' tank-like Oldsmobile.

"Sorry, Mom was running late. Too late to call you. I had to wait." She raised the hem of her red velvet dress to reveal four-inch heels. "Or walk, and in these, that was a no-go."

"Still, you should have called. I'd have driven out to get you."

"You're taking me home." She looped her arm through Ashley's. "Let's go do our chaperone thing."

"This chaperoning is another first for me."

"Piece of cake." Shannon laughed.

"What do we do?"

"Watch for liquor, stop the making out in dark corners, and keep counting the couples to be sure none of them slip out. Dr. Evans will be here. He and the male teachers usually patrol the parking lot."

"Not tonight."

At the sound of Tyler's voice, her heart rate jumped from zero to one-fifty in a sonic boom. Twirling around, she stiffened at the sight of him in a black suit and red necktie with Santa's sleigh peeking from the vee of the jacket. This was not high school Tyler Evans. He looked sophisticated and downright yummy in his holiday attire. Her racing blood pulsed siren warnings.

"What are you doing here?" Her voice came out all squeaky. Her knees wobbled.

"Dad's running a temperature and Mom's put him to bed. I'm filling in."

Or, more likely, their mothers were plotting again.

Ashley took one look at Tyler and came to full attention like a puppy spying her chew bone treat. "I don't believe we've met, I'm Ashley Hill. It's my first-year teaching English."

"Tyler Evans. Nice to meet you." He extended his hand to Ashley, holding it a little longer than Shannon thought necessary.

"I'm off to help the DJ set up his equipment. If y'all need anything holler."

Shannon shook her head. "We're good."

As he walked away, Ashley gave an approving nod. "So that's the infamous superintendent's son. Tell me again why it is you're not interested in that gorgeous hunk of manhood."

"I told you I can't afford any relationship." *Financially or emotionally.* Even as she finished that thought, she knew what her heart wanted. What it had always wanted before she got caught up in the excitement of bright city lights and a fast-paced life. Before Eric's lies and deceit. Tyler Evans owned her heart and being back here had solidified that truth.

Enough.

She might want to run to Tyler, grab him, and kiss him, she couldn't. Wouldn't. She had a good start untangling the mess of her life. She had some savings again, but she was a long way from making any commitments to another human.

"You go check on the refreshment table. Be sure no one's spiked the punch. I'm going to help at the sign-in table."

Chapter Eight

Tyler worked with the DJ, but his eyes followed Shannon. In that red dress with her auburn-red hair, she was like a flare. She'd worn a similar red dress to the Christmas prom when they'd been crowned King and Queen of the Winter Ball. He couldn't believe how much he missed her. It was a deep ache that started in his heart and spread to every nerve ending in his body.

"I'm ready to start playing." The DJ adjusted the mic and volume levels. "Any preference for the ratio of fast to slow tunes."

"I thought you DJ guys decided all that."

He flashed a sly smile. "Just checking. Principals never like two slow songs played together with all these teen hormones on overdrive tonight."

It wasn't only the teens. His libido was in high gear too.

"I can appreciate that." Tyler chuckled. "Let's go with that plan, but I have a specific request for the King and Queen dance if you have it available." He named the song as the gym filled with chatters and giggles of nervous and excited teenagers.

The DJ gave him a thumbs-up and lifted the mic to his lips. "Good evening, you gorgeous people. Let's get this party started."

With the push of a button, music blared from the gigantic speakers.

As the rush of arrivals slowed down, Shannon left the government teacher in charge of sign-in and walked around the edges of the cafeteria. She spotted Ashley and Tyler talking on the other side of the room. Another dart of jealousy stabbed her heart.

She looked away. A thousand brilliant points of pain exploded somewhere in the vicinity of her chest. The sounds from the gym fell away, leaving her in a vacuum filled with memories and silent remorse from long-ago mistakes.

She had no right to feel anything. She'd rejected him. He could be with anyone he pleased.

Holly and Brock danced past with a wave. They'd made up after that first disastrous football game. Shannon hoped the two of them could find the happily-ever-after she and Tyler had missed.

She circled the cafeteria greeting teachers and her girls, as she'd come to think of the drill team and cheerleaders. All the while keeping up with Tyler. She couldn't stop herself. That other Christmas prom kept cycling through her head. They'd been so happy and in love with plans to get married after college. Plans foiled by her foolishness.

Their eyes met. He held hers for a moment, smiling slowly. Her heart made a loop-the-loop and landed in her stomach as he came toward her.

Mr. Stone, the history teacher, stepped in front of her. "I think a chaperone is needed." He tipped his head toward a couple making out in the corner. "Want me to go?"

Transported back in time, a snapshot of her and Tyler in the same spot at their senior prom flashed in her head and tinted her cheeks. Mr. Stone had been chaperoning that night too.

That poor couple didn't need the same memory. "Nah. I've got it."

"How you doing, Mr. Stone? Still on patrol, I sec," Tyler said as he joined them. His cheek twitched as if he was struggling to hold his grin.

Shannon whirled around and made her way to break up the couple.

With a couple of hours left, Ashley waved Shannon over to her table. She slid into the chair and toed off her shoes. "My feet are dying. I rarely wear heels."

"Mine too. It's why I wear flats for teaching. At least you get to wear tennis shoes when you work."

"And I love it. How're you liking your first Christmas prom chaperoning?"

"Easier than I thought. The kids are being good, for the most part. I saw you talking to the couple in the corner. I stopped a couple heading to their car." She winked. "They said she left something in the car, but we know that's not what they were going for."

"Does bring back fond memories." Tyler pulled out a chair and joined them.

Ashley looked from one to the other. "That's right. I've heard stories about you two high school sweethearts."

"Kinda feels weird to be on this side of things. Don't you think, Shannon?"

"Yes weird, and it was a long time ago." Only it didn't feel so long ago tonight. She shifted her gaze away and did a sweeping look around the room.

Conversation faded as the trio watched the teenagers dancing. The next song ended with Holly and Brock standing in front of their table. "I bet Mr. Evans would dance if you asked him, Ms. O'Leary." Holly gave an exaggerated wink.

"Or you could dance with me." Brock held out his hand.

"I'd love to, Brock. Thanks for asking." Anything to get away from Tyler and the memories.

Brock placed his hand at her waist and held her

at arm's length as if dancing a Victorian-era waltz as the music filled the air.

"This is an oldie special for all you alumni here tonight. Debbie Gibson's *Lost in Your Eyes*," the DJ announced.

The first couple of notes sent a chill down Shannon's spine. Of all the songs.

Before she and Brock took a step, Tyler tapped on Brock's shoulder. "Mind if I cut in? This song's an old favorite of ours."

"No, sir, not at all. I'd hate to waste a slow one on a teacher." Brock's arm fell away from Shannon and encircled Holly's waist. He pulled her close. She rested her cheek in the hollow of his shoulder and they danced away.

Tyler tugged Shannon into his embrace. "I'm glad they've patched up their differences."

His hand tightened around her waist. How could he make small talk while her world just shifted on its axis?

She had to get a grip on her emotions.

"They do make a handsome couple, but does anyone really know what they want at seventeen or eighteen?"

"I did," he whispered and executed a perfect dip then pulled her even closer.

Her cheeks might have just gone purple. She couldn't see them, but her face sure burned with fire. Without thinking, she burrowed her nose into his chest so no one could see.

Tyler slid his hand to the middle of her back, squeezing her even tighter. That sent another rush of unwelcome heat.

What was he doing? No way he could still have feelings for her after all that she'd put him through. Confusion muddled her thoughts. She had to stop this madness.

Not wanting to make a scene, she pushed away slowly, gently. "I don't think this sets a very good example," she said in her best teacher's voice.

"I'm not doing anything that half the guys on the floor aren't doing." He flashed a lethal smile that made her nearly swallow her tongue.

Shannon looked around. He was right. "Well, we all need a cool down." She straightened her shoulders and arched to face him. "Isn't it time to announce the Winter King and Queen? You ready to MC?"

Anything so he wasn't touching her.

"Ready." His cheeks rose in the proverbial cat swallowed the canary grin. She could almost see the yellow feather between his lips.

What was he up to?

He tugged her toward the DJ table on the raised platform. The music stopped. The DJ handed him the microphone. Shannon stood frozen beside him.

Tyler tapped the mike. "Time to crown our Christmas Prom king and queen. For those of you who don't know me, I'm Tyler Evans. Dr. Evan's son and a former Winter King and, you all know Ms. O'Leary." He swept his arm her way. "Who just happened to be my queen that night."

Catcalls drowned out the rest of his words. Shouts of "Tyler and Shannon" echoed through the gym.

Shannon cringed. All those Tyler and Shannon stories passed around while they decorated for the dance had obviously spread over the whole school population.

Tyler tapped the mic again. "I know how much some of you have been waiting for this moment." He waved the winner's envelope, quieting the crowd. "This year's King and Queen are. . ." With all the flair of an Academy Award presenter, he ripped the envelope open. The room went quiet.

"And the winners are... Brock Walters and Holly Hempstead. Congratulations, guys."

Wolf whistles and applause erupted again. Brock and Holly came on stage. Shannon placed the capes around their shoulders while Tyler handed them their scepters then moved to stand behind them, "Dawson Springs High School Cougars, I present to you, King Brock and Queen Holly."

Brock and Holly clasped hands and faced the others. More cheers rose.

"And now with King Brock's permission, I'd like to ask my former Queen to join me in the first dance of your reign." He bowed low. "That be okay, my king?"

"What? Wait. No. This isn't how it's supposed to be." Shannon stuttered through each word.

"Go for it, sir," Brock said.

"Absolutely," Holly echoed.

Tyler motioned to the DJ. "If you please."

Following Brock and Holly, Tyler led her onto the dance floor and twirled Shannon into his arms.

Time and space faded as memory carried her back to that other time when they were the most popular couple in high school and so deeply in love. There was no yesterday, no regret, no mistakes.

Tyler cupped her hand in his against his broad chest. She heard his heart beating as fast as hers.

The lights dimmed. The music started. Spotlights centered on current and past kings and their queens following their perfectly matched steps. How wonderful and safe she felt in his arms. Why had she tossed it all away?

She wished the dance could go on forever. But they didn't have forever. She'd messed that up for good. This was just a trip down memory lane. She had to snap out of it before she made a fool of herself.

She glanced over his shoulder at the gym clock. Forty more minutes. That's all she had to get through. She willed the warm memories and feelings away, determined to focus on her duties. She scanned the gym and spied a couple disappearing into the hall. The chaperon thing had worked before, so why not hide behind work again?

As the dance ended, she asked Tyler to check on the disappearing couple while she went to interrupt another couple making out against the far wall. She left so quickly he didn't have a chance to say a word.

Chapter Nine

*B*y midnight, the gym was empty. All the tables and chairs collapsed and, along with the platform and props, returned to the storage area. The custodian swept glitter off the floor. Shannon retrieved her purse and met Tyler and Ashley in the parking lot.

"Change of plans. I told Ashley I'd give you a ride home since her place is in the opposite direction." Tyler's eyes never left Shannon's.

Ashley gave her a sheepish grin. "I said great. I hope that's okay. We'll talk tomorrow. It was a great night."

It's not okay.

"Thanks for your help tonight." She hugged Ashley.

After Ashley climbed into her car, Shannon turned to Tyler. "I'll call Mom and Dad. One of them can come."

I can't ride home with you.

"I already called them. They know I'm bringing you home."

Of course, he did, and there went her last hope of escape. She expelled a hefty sigh. "You talked to them?"

"I figured you'd balk and gave them a heads up. Your mom thought it was a wonderful idea."

Of course, she would."

"Tyler, this is not a good idea."

"I'm not asking you to elope. It's just a ride home."

"And you, we, need to remember that. Since you've eliminated my options, guess I have no choice."

Tyler laughed aloud and clasped his hands over his chest like he had been wounded. "It's not a death sentence you know." He linked his arm through hers and moved toward the only car left in the student parking area, a Cadillac Escalade.

"This is your car? I thought—"

"What? That I was a poor, starving artist that only drove the same beat-up pickup from when we'd dated? Things have changed. The truck's for work." He supported her arm as she climbed inside.

"I didn't mean to sound so surprised. It's just I … I didn't know you'd done so well." She leaned back on the buttery soft leather headrest. Once again, she'd sold him short. "I apologize."

"No apology necessary. The Caddy's for special occasions. Like your Bessie, my truck is perfect for my local house painting jobs." With a wink, he closed her door and rounded the hood to climb behind the driver's seat.

"Wait. So that land where we had the picnic was yours?" she asked as the dashboard came to life like the cockpit of a jetliner.

"Yep. I'll take you to see the house one of these days." His eyes sparkled in the starlight when he looked over at her. "If you want."

"I'd like that." He'd stayed in Dawson Springs and made good while she'd left and failed. Fate sure had a weird sense of humor. "So, tell me about your work.

"You know all I ever wanted to do was paint." He looked over at her. "Besides you, that is."

"Tyler don't start. That was a very long time ago."

"Doesn't feel that way to me. Tonight, you in that dress and the music made it feel like it was yesterday."

"Don't worry, by tomorrow morning this night will be gone and everything will be back to normal." A part of her prayed her words were true. "Now tell me about your art."

"My football scholarship paid for art school, as you know. After that, the pickings were lean. I did some freelance work for greeting cards and murals, all the time building my portfolio and networking with the art community. House painting paid the bills. Then I met an older woman who owned an art studio in Austin. She offered to feature some of my paintings in a show."

Tyler paused and rolled his head over his shoulder to stretch his neck. He sucked in his bottom lip like he was uncomfortable with this part of the story.

Her mother had hinted he'd been with an older woman for a while. "Let me guess. She loved your art, but she liked you too?"

"Something like that. But nothing happened, I swear."

She held her hands up. "Hey, no judging. I've made far too many mistakes in my life to cast shadows."

"As it turned out," he continued. "I sold several paintings and made contacts with other studio owners in places like Colorado, New York, and Arizona. After that, I was launched. And she moved on to her next prodigy."

She reached across the console and squeezed his arm. "I'm so glad things worked out for you."

"And I'm sorry you've had such a hard go of it. I wish you'd tell me how I can help." He slowed to turn into Irish Oaks' entrance. This time he drove over the cattle guard slowly and shifted his head her way with a sheepish grin and a wink. "See. things can change."

Tyler pulled to a stop in front of the house and turned to face her. "What happened, Shannon? I know about divorce but there's more, right? Maybe I can help."

"I don't think so." She reached for the handle.

He leaned over and stopped her gently. "Don't go. Talk to me."

Tears hovered in the corner of her eyes before slipping down her cheek. "I don't know how. I'm so embarrassed at the mess I've made."

"Trust me. Please. No judging." His thumb rubbed the inside of her elbow offering the promise of friendship.

Besides being her first love, Tyler had been her best friend. She used to share things with him. She wanted to trust him again, to tell him what a fool she'd been. Her heart broke a little more at the possibility that after she did, he'd find her so ridiculous he'd leave and never look back.

"I've done a lot of stupid things."

"Hey. Look at me." He tipped her chin up in his direction and swiped away the tear on her cheek. "We've all done silly things. I won't think anything but how glad I am that we can talk again."

"Okay, come in and I'll fix us a cup of coffee."

He followed her up the porch stairs and into the kitchen. With familiarity, Shannon filled the coffee maker with water while he slid his jacket onto the back of the chrome chair then went to the cabinet for the mugs and coffee canister.

Kicking off her shoes, she sat at the table to wait for the coffeemaker to do its thing. "My feet are killing me."

A weak stall tactic, but this wasn't going to be easy.

He slid his chair in front of hers and lifted her foot into his lap. "I love how you look in them but I do understand why women think they're instruments of torture." His fingers worked circles on the ball of her foot. "That better?"

"Much." It was more than better and sparked thoughts she had no right to think.

"Tell me what happened." Tyler's smooth hand inched up to work her ankle and calves. Heat snaked through her body. She should pull away. She simply couldn't.

"I got to the city and Eric showed me a side of life I'd never seen. I liked it. He made it seem like a fairy tale and I got taken in by his charm." She'd been too naïve to see through Eric and realize how foolish she was being by not listening to her family's warnings and too quick to cast Tyler aside. She'd hurt so many.

The gurgling stopped and the scent of freshly brewed coffee filled the air. She slipped her foot to the floor and went to the counter. Filling the mugs, she added one sugar and a drop of cream to Tyler's before returning to the table.

He took a sip. "Just the way I like it. You remembered."

Her chin dropped and her hands cupped her coffee mug before lifting her gaze to meet his. "I remember a lot."

With a discreet smile, he reached down and took her other foot in his lap. "Go on with your story. I promise no judging."

Despite his words, she was afraid exposing how stupid she'd been might kill whatever good feelings he still had for her.

His touch was soothing as he worked the tired muscles in her foot and calf. She sipped her coffee letting herself luxuriate in his touch. "That feels so wonderful. I don't ever want you to stop."

"Oh no, you don't, Shannon. You're stalling. I deserve to know what happened." The foot massage stopped. His hands dropped away. All the warmth of his touch evaporated. Pain filled his eyes, and it crushed her heart knowing she'd put it there.

She leaned forward, cupped his cheek. "If only I —"

His hand covered hers. "We can fix this."

She pushed to the back of the chair, straightening her spine, and prayed he was right.

With a remorseful sigh, she began. "When I finished my internship at Eric's gym, he offered me a job. We started dating. That part you know. Everything went well the first couple of years. I wondered about his parents who were never around.

They didn't even come to our wedding. Eric always had a plausible excuse. They were off in some exotic place or something. Turns out, they'd disowned him because he squandered his inheritance from his grandmother. Eric liked the finer things."

She paused and searched the black depths of her mug for strength, pausing to take a sip. "I foolishly wanted all those things too in the beginning. We started struggling financially, so I took a job teaching. The salary barely paid our bills. During summers I worked as the children's class instructor at our gym, and during the school year, I taught kids' gymnastic classes on weekends and after school. My days were long but I enjoyed the kids. I quit buying things. Eric didn't."

She fortified herself with another sip of coffee, watching Tyler.

He picked up her foot and started massaging again. "Go on."

"Eric spent more and more time at the gym and less and less time at home. I could hardly keep up with my schedule, and, I guess, a part of me hoped his absence meant he was working with more clients to help dig us out of our hole. I didn't want to think about him being unfaithful, but the signs were there. My head-in-the-sand act ended abruptly when I caught him with one of his private training clients on a bench in the women's locker room."

She pulled her foot from Tyler's lap and propped her elbows on the table, shaking. "I thought she was *my* friend, and she wasn't the first, just one of many. I kicked him out."

Tyler slammed his palm on the table hard, loudly. "What an absolute slimeball."

"It gets worse. When I started canceling joint bank and credit card accounts, I discovered my bigger problem. Eric had spent us into six-figure debt."

"Wow. That's a lot of expensive stuff."

"I know. I might not have been able to stop the affairs, but the financial wreck was as much my fault as his. I let him manage all our finances and never questioned."

She ran her hands up and down her arms. Her eyes clouded with remembered guilt. So much she should have done.

He reached out and put his hand where her arms crossed, stopping the movement. "But once you figured it out, you did something."

"Too little too late." Pushing away, she went to refill her mug. "You want more?" He shook his head.

She carried her mug back to the table and sat for a minute before going on. She couldn't look at Tyler. "He'd forged my signature on a loan against my CDs. That's where I'd banked my inheritance from Aunt Tillie."

"Holy cow. That's a federal offense."

"I know, and that's when I went to his parents and threatened to file charges." She took a deep breath. "Knowing how they'd disowned him before

I was afraid, they'd say let him go to jail. But they didn't want the family name disgraced and agreed to help a little. We sold our house, our cars, and the business. I filed for divorce and walked away broke. They only covered the loss from the sale of the house. Said it was a good lesson to learn. And they weren't wrong."

Her shoulders rose and fell in a defeated sigh. "On a teacher's salary it'll be years before I'm able to afford a new car and a place to live. To really start my life again."

"I could give you an interest-free loan."

After the way she'd hurt him, she couldn't believe he'd be so generous. "Thank you. Dad offered too. I love you both for wanting to help, but I made this mess. I need to fix it myself."

Tyler took his mug to the counter then returned to stand behind her. His fingers worked the tight muscles in her shoulders and neck. "You're being too hard on yourself. Let me help so we can get on with *our* lives."

She stood to face him. "But I'd always know you paid my debt. I couldn't live with that. It's no way to start a relationship."

"Shannon, it's only money. I have plenty." He pulled her into his arms. "I don't have you. I've never stopped loving you. I want us to be together. I'm pretty sure that's what you want too."

He pressed his lips against hers. His fingers combed through her hair as he deepened the kiss. In the space of a heartbeat, she lost control, wrapping her arms around his waist and returning the kiss with equal fervor.

"I do love you too," she whispered against his lips.

Empty, the coffee maker sent up a burning smell, breaking the spell. Her hands slid to his chest between them, pushing him away. "But we can't do this. I'm sorry."

She picked up the mugs and put them in the sink. She didn't deserve this man who so quickly forgave her for leaving him and *still* loved her. But she couldn't allow him to solve her problem as easy as that would be.

Chapter Ten

Tyler clinched his teeth and counted to ten letting the lingering cinnamon scent from her mom's Christmastime candle calm his frustration. "You are so stubborn. I want to help."

"Please understand. I screwed this up, and I won't have anyone fixing it for me."

He clamped his back teeth, letting her words fade then whipped his jacket from the chair. "It's settled then."

But he wasn't going to let this go. She'd said she loved him. There had to be a way for them to be together.

"I'll be leaving for a gallery opening in Arizona this week then from there I go to a show in Colorado. I'll be home for Christmas at your folks'."

"Okay. I'd like that."

He gave her another kiss, confident that their old holiday tradition and so much more would once again be in place. His steps bounced as he went to his car.

Shannon never thought her heart could ever feel this way again. Or that being back in Dawson Springs would be so good. She'd returned with her tail between her legs determined to sock away as much money as she could and get out of Dodge again as fast as she could.

Instead she'd found friendship and a sense of home she never expected and discovered living in small-town Dawson Springs suited her just fine.

Could it be she wasn't such a big-city girl after all? Staring out her bedroom window at Venus, she dared to think of all the possibilities of a life with Tyler. To make wishes for their happily ever after.

The logical part of her couldn't believe he still loved her after hearing her story. But Tyler said he did. He wasn't Eric. She could trust his word.

More importantly, he'd wait until she was ready. He'd already waited. She wrapped her arms around her chest with a deep, contented sigh. *He loved her.* How had she gotten so lucky?

She didn't hear from him while he was away. It was just as well. In his arms, her heart overflowed while her brain whispered all the possibilities of what a life with him would be like. His absence let her think logically, and unfortunately, she couldn't see a way around her money problem. As sure as she was of her love for him and his for her, she wouldn't risk not being able to take care of herself again. She dreaded facing him on Christmas Day and explaining.

At the same time, she couldn't wait to be with him.

With their Christmas Day tradition back, their moms were going to push even harder for the future they wanted for them. They'd have to understand.

He'd have to understand.

Until she was on her feet financially, they had no future.

On Christmas morning carols played softly, a spread with sweets suited for royalty lined the buffet, and tiny white lights made starbursts sparkle off the glass ornaments on the massive tree. She and her dad had cut it down like they had every Christmas when she lived at home.

It was all perfect.

"Sweetheart, will you help me?" Her mother tilted her head toward the kitchen where the aroma of brown sugar and mustard-based ham floated in the air.

Shannon headed into the large bright room that was the heart of their home. "What can I do?"

Her mom wrapped her in a tight hug and held on. "I want you to believe, my little one."

"Believe? I don't understand. In what?"

"Miracles. I've seen how you've been moping around since the Christmas Prom. Did something happen? I heard you and Tyler down here talking late into the night when he brought you home."

"He told me he still loves me, Mom. I can't believe it after the way I jilted him. But unless I can get on my feet financially again, we can't be together."

"I understand. Eric's broken your trust, but Tyler's not Eric. Christmas is a time of miracles. You've just forgotten how to believe in them." Her mom took a step back and held Shannon's hands. "Life is full of curveballs, and not all of them are bad. Give Tyler a chance."

Her mom hugged her again and the day felt full of possibilities.

The doorbell sounded and voices floated into the kitchen. "They're here. It's going to be a perfect Christmas." Her mom dashed off grinning like a little kid whose best friend had come to play.

Shannon lingered behind, not ready to face the others or the memories. Squaring her shoulders, she stepped to the doorway a minute later.

Her eyes found Tyler first. He wore a red and

green plaid shirt with jeans and cowboy boots. Muscles filled out the western shirt and stretched his sleeves in all the right places. He looked as good as—no better than—he had in his suit and tie prom night.

Watching him laugh at something her dad said tugged at her battered heart. *Forget your silly pride!* shouted in her head.

In the back of her heart, on the tip of her brain, she recognized this man would always put her first. But the reality of all she'd been through held her firm.

His eyes danced as they met hers and his cheeks curved in a wry smile. She returned the smile and prayed for that Christmas miracle her mom believed in.

Chapter Eleven

"Welcome home. How did your shows go?" Shannon greeted him. His ears treasured the sound and he longed for the day he'd hear them whenever he came home.

"Fantastic. Everything I'd hoped for and more." Tyler wanted to scoop her into his arms and shout his good news. He forced self-control.

"Come on you two. This ham's getting cold," her dad called from the dining room.

Shannon took his hand and led the way to the table. Her hand was soft and smooth, and wow did the feel of it ever do wild things to his insides.

After the blessing, serving dishes circled the table. Mashed potatoes, brussels sprouts cooked in bacon, sweet potatoes, green bean casserole, dressing, fruit salad... a feast that would generate leftovers for days. He'd missed this. Dreamed about it since he'd heard she'd divorced. He reached and gave Shannon's hand another squeeze to reassure himself he wasn't dreaming.

Conversation flowed as if there hadn't been a five-year gap in the gatherings. He kept stealing glances at Shannon. He'd missed her on his trip, but he hadn't called. He didn't want to push her. He'd said his piece prom night and she hers. He understood. Even in high school she'd wanted to be independent. What happened with her marriage only reinforced that.

He could be patient. Like he'd been with the stray dumped at his studio. It had taken him months to convince the abused dog he wasn't going to hurt him. But he'd won Picasso over and he'd win back Shannon's heart too.

"That was delicious, ladies. I may have eaten too much," his dad said.

"Me, too." Shannon's dad nodded. "I could use a nap."

Bud Evans pushed from the table and rubbed his belly. "You can have the couch. I'll stretch out on the guest room bed like I used to do."

No, no, no. A mild panic seized Tyler. They had to open the presents next. He'd waited long enough.

Shannon's mom laughed. "We all ate too much. But no napping. You're supposed to move around after a big meal. Bud, go with Liam to check the baby calf while Jean and I clear the dishes. And don't be gone long. We're gonna be opening presents next."

Tyler wanted to kiss her mom.

Shannon offered to help in the kitchen. "It'll go faster with more hands. Tyler you can go with the guys."

He'd rather stay with her, but he followed the two men to the coat rack and trudged behind. He'd waited this long, what was an hour more?

With the dishwasher loaded and the leftovers sorted, Shannon's mom led the way to the living room. "I texted Liam. The guys should be here any minute."

When all the coats and hats hung on the coat rack by the back door, Shannon passed out the gifts and waited patiently while the others opened theirs. Then it was Tyler's turn. She handed him the book of paintings by famous artists she'd found at a used bookstore. Her meager gift could never compare to whatever was inside that fancy-wrapped box he'd put under the tree for her.

After opening the book, he leafed through the pages. "I love it. It'll inspire me."

"And this is for you." He walked to the tree and lifted the large, very lightweight box.

She held her breath knowing all eyes were on her as she ripped the paper away. Inside were two pieces of paper. One was a receipt for the sale of a 30" x 35" oil painting titled "Shannon" and the other a cashier's check made out to her with more zeroes than she'd seen since looking at the sum of debt Eric accumulated.

"I don't understand."

Tyler scooted closer. "Like I told you, I displayed it as an example of my portrait work. A man at the Phoenix show has bugged me for years to sell your painting to him. I didn't because it wasn't mine to sell. I'd given it to you."

"You mean the one of Shannon on the porch swing?" Shannon's mother asked. "I loved it."

Tyler nodded. "That's the one."

"But you said you'd never ever sell it." His mother sounded dumbfounded.

"I don't understand either. You could have sold it at any time. I gave it back to you."

"I know, but I always felt like it belonged to you."

"Why'd you change your mind and sell it, son?" Shannon's dad asked.

"In a recent discussion Shannon said she didn't want it because... well that's not important. Once she said she didn't want it back, I knew whatever I sold it for would be hers. She'd be able to solve her money problems and solving that would mean we could be together." He smiled at her. "I made plans to meet the man at the Phoenix show who been asking to buy it for years. I promise I'll paint another one for you."

Shannon sat too stunned to speak for long

seconds. Hope, joy, and love swirled within her chest until she thought she'd burst. "I can't believe it."

"How much?" her mom asked.

"Mom!"

Tyler grinned. "You'll have to ask Shannon. The check's made out to her."

"It's your Christmas miracle." She passed the check to her mom. Her eyes popped wide when she read the amount.

"Of course, it is, sweetheart. You just had to believe." She returned the check to Shannon.

Tears filled her eyes as Shannon looked from the check to Tyler. Never in her wildest dreams could she have imagined this. Their conversation after the Christmas prom ran through her head. The check was truly hers. She could pay off her credit cards, buy a used car, and put a deposit on a place of her own with change.

She hugged this man who loved her despite her mistakes, despite all the hurt she'd caused him. "Thank you," she whispered as tears of happiness trailed down her cheeks.

"I do have something else." He slipped his hand into his pocket and dropped to his knee. His gaze never left hers as he lifted the lid of a little black velvet box slowly. "I've held onto this too. Shannon O'Leary, I have never not loved you and I will never stop loving you. Will you marry me?"

"Yes, yes, yes," she whispered over the lump in her throat, and from behind her, their parents cheered.

Chapter Twelve

Six months later...

Ashley helped Shannon adjust the ivory Irish lace Mantilla that had belonged to her Aunt Tillie. "You look so gorgeous. Tyler is going to be blown away."

"I hope so." She smoothed the simple ivory gown she'd chosen over a traditional formal wedding dress over her hips. Eric had insisted she wear an expensive designer gown for their wedding.

Tyler wanted to buy her one too. She said no.

This time money and things didn't matter to her. Back then she'd thought designer gowns and wealth was what she wanted. No more.

"I know he will be." Ashley faced her in the

standing mirror. "I've never seen you look so radiant."

She blinked back a tear. "Thank you. I truly never thought this would happen."

"Ashley's right. You look gorgeous." Her mother beamed. "And happy again."

Shannon stared into the mirror. She was happy. She may have been forced to abandon her plans and return to Dawson Springs, but she was happier than she'd ever been. She'd come to appreciate the things she'd taken for granted before and to recognize one big important fact. Plans change and it's not always a bad thing.

A tap on the door signaled it was time to head to the sanctuary where her father, and Tyler, waited. She squeezed her mother's hand.

"Let's do this." Ashley waved her on.

"You're next," Shannon said as she went through the doorway.

"Gotta find the right guy first like you did."

Shannon grinned. "You will."

Tyler stood at the altar with his eyes glued to the end of the church aisle. His knees went weak when Shannon stepped through on her dad's arm.

He'd all but given up hope that this moment would happen. Now, all his heart had ever needed was coming toward him. Her gaze met with his, never wavering. He locked the vision in his head. That was how he was going to paint his new picture of her.

Her father lifted her hand and placed it in Tyler's. She squeezed his hand. "I love you forever."

"Forever," he echoed as they turned toward the minister.

Acknowledgments

Thanks to the best critique/writing partners ever for helping me push this out there.

And extra special hugs and thanks to the role model for all my heroes, my most trusted story editor, and eagle-eyed copy editor. Love you, always and forever, JMH.

Author's Note

Dear Reader,

Thank you so much for reading Christmas Prom Rerun. If you enjoyed Shannon and Tyler's story, please help others find and enjoy the book, too.

Word of mouth is incredibly important for helping others discover authors. Recommend this book to friends, readers' groups, and discussion boards so other readers can find it. Take a moment to write a review or give a star-rank on GoodReads or Amazon.

If you'd like to make sure you never miss a new release, sign up for my newsletter at https://judythcmorgan.com/ and please like my Facebook page at https://www.facebook.com/JudytheMorgan/

Continue reading for an excerpt from, ***Dead Body Girl***

Until next time!
Judythe

Dead Body Girl
Romantic Suspense Based on a True Event

judythe morgan

Chapter One

The ribbon of road wound through the soft foothills of northeast Virginia, winding and twisting like the Shenandoah River that threaded through the area. Scents of spring whipped inside the open truck window and anticipation filled MaryDee Ross. Early morning dew sparkled in the rising sun of the April morning. Too cool for the heater, not yet warm enough for air-conditioning. Sometimes these farm sales were Aladdin's cave, other times a trash dump. Either way, estate sales were the lifeblood of her antique shop.

She spotted the sale sign marking the turn on a familiar road close to where she lived. She headed over the covered bridge. The same one she and her younger sister Claudia had ridden their bikes over in hopes of spotting Gus whose family farm was only a little further down the two-lane road. Until— Nope. Not going there.

She squeezed the steering wheel until the veins in her hand popped. The rhythmic click of her tires over the wooden planks. She refocused to see dozens of cars pulled off the road at various angles.

People wandered through the assortment of items spread around the yard. Others trailed inside the barn and up the porch stairs into the house. Wishing she'd spent a little less time over her morning tea, she guided her pickup off the road, hopped out, and powerwalked to the clapboard farmhouse she'd always admired from the road.

The front porch overflowed with furniture—oak tables, enamel top kitchen tables, marble tops, pie safes, China cabinets, and dozens of assorted chairs. MaryDee scooted between pieces pausing long enough to examine things that caught her dealer's eye. Around the corner on the side porch, she spotted a Hoosier cabinet. One of her clients wanted a vintage baking center.

She tucked her elbows close, squeezed between people to examine the piece. When she opened one of the cabinet doors, someone shoved against the cabinet door from the other side. "Excuse me. You're blocking the aisle."

"Sorry." MaryDee swung the door closed and stared into the face of her sister's former mother-in-law, Willa Nolan. A lump the size of Mount

Vernon filled her throat, blocking her air, and stole the moisture from her mouth. "Mima? I mean, Ms. Nolan?"

"MaryDee. I'm so happy to see you." The flabby skin below the elderly woman's biceps swayed as she scooped MaryDee into one of her "Mima" hugs. The hairspray-stiff hair scratched MaryDee's forehand and the familiar scent of Hermes Caleche filled her nostrils. The woman used to one of her best customers and bought every bottle of the sixties vintage scent she'd found.

Another thing Claudia had cost her.

"Let's go find someplace where we can catch up."

Before she could politely refuse, Mima slipped her arm through MaryDee's and guided her off the porch toward a group of wrought iron chairs beneath a sprawling sweetgum tree in the yard. Mima settled onto the loveseat, pointing to a chair.

MaryDee looked around. "I'm not sure we should be sitting here. Sellers don't like it when you mess with their stuff."

Mima flapped her hands in dismissal. "I've bought it. So, sit. Tell me how you've been."

MaryDee fidgeted unsure what was happening. Mima hadn't spoken to her in eight years ago. "I'm good. But I should check out that Hoosier." She started to stand.

"Sit. It's not going anywhere. Darlene wants too much for it."

"You know the seller?" Silly question. The

matriarch of their county knew everyone and everything that went on.

"Sister-in-law. I tried to tell her to contact you about doing the estate sale for her. Now that she sees this mad house, she wishes she has."

"I would have loved to talk with her." MaryDee started to stand again. "I need to examine that Hoosier before someone else snatches it up. I have a client that wants one."

"Keep your pants on." Mima pulled her phone from her purse. "Darlene, it's Willa. I want the Hoosier too. Okay. Thanks." She smiled at MaryDee and slid her phone back into her purse. "Done."

"But what if my client doesn't want it?"

"I'll consign it to you. Enough about that. I want to know what's been going on with you."

MaryDee's head spun like a merry-go-round. She toed an arch in the grass with her shoe. "I lost some come customers after ... you know ... but business is steady and building again."

"I apologize. What happened wasn't your fault. I've missed you and your shop."

Hadn't she always been blamed for Claudia's messes? Thousands of miles away Claudia remained completely oblivious to the destruction she'd left in her wake.

"I've missed you, too. You were my best customer, and picker."

Mima's shoulders dipped in a heavy sigh. "Gus tells me all the time I shouldn't have blamed you."

Her heart froze for a second. "He's in Virginia?"

Mima's gaze shifted over MaryDee's shoulder and gave a nod.

Taking a deep breath, MaryDee turned. Gus strolled toward them. Slow and easy. His shoulders relaxed, his steps sure. Older, streaks of grey now peppered his sideburns, but still six feet of toned muscle. He didn't make eye contact yet every cell in her body tingled.

"MaryDee." He tipped his head her way and sat beside his grandmother. His eyes, the color of black tea, settled on her. "How have you been?"

His tone wasn't cold, but formal, professional, an interrogation voice. She'd heard Detective Harrison use the same when talking to witnesses. MaryDee bit her bottom lip. "Fine. Just fine."

She took Mima's hand in hers. "I need to get back to my looking before all the good stuff is gone. I hope to see you in the shop again soon."

"You can count on it, honey. And I'll get Darlene to call you. She's gonna have a ton of stuff left after the sale." She flashed a generous smile.

A corner turned, MaryDee thought, having Mima back. Gus, she wasn't so sure. Why was he here?

Gus gave MaryDee's retreat a long steady survey. He saw pieces of the girl he'd known, cared for, but she'd changed. Stronger, sharper than before. Her sister might not overpower her so much anymore.

"Gus! Are you listening?" Mima's voice penetrated his thoughts. "I swear to goodness your brain's a mess since you got back. Pay attention."

His brain was a mess. Only it wasn't just what happened in South America or this new assignment. MaryDee'd always messed with his head.

"I was. You want this iron yard loaded. Then... hmm, okay, maybe I drifted off some. Show me what else."

MaryDee pulled into the parking space beside her shop in the small retail center on Route 50. When the space became available, she'd jumped at the chance to sign a lease and move from her booths in an antique mall miles away.

Kaley opened the shop's door for her. "Looks like you had a good run."

"I did. There's more in the truck." She carried the overflowing box to the sales counter.

Kaley followed with another. One by one MaryDee lined items on the 1900s feedstore counter that served for checkout. "And best news, I found a Hoosier I think the Crawfords will love. It's being delivered."

"A good run indeed. See any dealers you knew?"

"About everyone. The place was packed." She lifted a lamp, examined the base for a mark. "Mima was there."

Kaley's hand stilled. She stared. "And?"

"We talked a bit."

"About time you two ended this silliness."

MaryDee nodded. "Gus was there, too."

"Really. How'd that go?"

"Well, he didn't stab me and I didn't stab him."

"That is progress."

Sign up for my newsletter at
https://judythemorgan.com/
to be notified of the release date.

About the Author

After years of roaming as an Air Force daughter and then Army wife, Texas called me home. My husband and I live in a small town called Rose Hill.

We raised three children, six Old English sheepdogs, one rescue terrier mix, and a Maltese. We have eleven grandchildren, three great-grandchildren, and nine granddogs who fill our lives with fun and laughter.

I've worked as a Department of Army civilian employee, a schoolteacher, an antique dealer (still am), a former mayor's wife, and sometimes a church pianist. Now I write full time.

All those crazy, and unique experiences fill my books with interesting twists and turns. My stories feature strong characters tackling real-life situations from a Christian worldview. I believe books should be a break from real life and leave you feeling happy.

Besides fiction, I share a weekly blog with my urban farmer/music teacher daughter at www. judythewriter.com

Sign up for my free newsletter at https://judythemorgan.com/ to keep up with my latest news and subscriber-only sneak peeks.

Follow me on :
Facebook
Amazon Author Page
BookBub
Goodreads

Also by Judythe

The Fitzpatrick Family Series
Eight preacher kids, each with a sweet romance story of their own.

Book 1, When Love Blooms
Book 2, When Love Returns
Book 3, When Love Endures
Book 4, When Love Trusts
Book 5, When Love Wins
Book 6, When Love Comes Home

Seeing Clearly
Thrilling suspense and seasoned romance

Ex-cop Dawson McKey is consumed by revenge after a cartel's bomb kills his twin sons. He trusts no one and vows payback. He refuses to get close to anyone, let alone fall in love again. But widow Evie Parker challenges his thinking. She's raising her grandson after her only child and his wife die in a suspicious car accident and it's taking a toll.

Alarms go off in Dawson's head when Evie receives threatening emails concerning her grandson. Then Evie's nanny disappears with her grandson. Dawson knows something is deadly wrong.

Pushed to their limits searching for the toddler, will Dawson and Evie learn seeing clearly is the only way to live and love?

Claiming Annie's Heart
An Irish Love Story

Annie Foster stays in Ireland after boarding school to nanny a widower's infant daughter. Five years later, the widower proposes.

Her first love Chad Jones, whom she believes abandoned her, arrives weeks before the wedding on an undercover assignment probing her fiancé's connection with IRA terrorists. Chad's determined to change Annie's mind and her heart because he's never stopped loving her.

Which man will claim Annie's heart?

The Promise Series

Two men and one woman met at Eighth Army Headquarters, South Korea in the turbulent Vietnam War years and their lives are irreversibly linked. The promises they made to themselves and each other bind their hearts forever.

Book 1, Love in the Morning Calm
Book 2, The Pendant's Promise
Book 3, Until He Returns
Book 4, Promises to Keep